This Topsy and Tim
book belongs to

All Ladybird books are available at most bookshops, supermarkets
and newsagents, or can be ordered direct from:
Ladybird Postal Sales PO Box 133 Paignton TQ3 2YP England
Telephone: (+44) 01803 554761   *Fax:* (+44) 01803 663394
A catalogue record for this book is available from the British Library

Published by Ladybird Books Ltd
A subsidiary of the Penguin Group
A Pearson Company
© Jean and Gareth Adamson MCMXCV
This edition MCMXCIX

The moral rights of the author/illustrator have been asserted
LADYBIRD and the device of a Ladybird are trademarks of Ladybird Books Ltd Loughborough Leicestershire UK

first school stories

Jean and Gareth Adamson

Contents

in the gym

Topsy and Tim were playing in the garden with their friend Josie Miller. Suddenly, Josie turned a cartwheel.

'I bet I can do that,' said Topsy.
'Me too,' said Tim. 'It's easy.' But it wasn't.
'I can do somersaults and handstands too,' said Josie. And she did.
Topsy and Tim wanted to know how.

Josie tried to teach Topsy and Tim.
It was hard work.
'I go to Gym Club,' said Josie at last.
'Why don't you come?'
Mummy thought it was a good idea.
'Perhaps they have a beginners' class,'
she said.

The next day after school, Topsy and
Tim and Mummy went with Josie to the
Leisure Centre. They sat and watched
Josie and her friends doing gymnastics.
'I'd like to do that,' said Tim, watching
a big boy bouncing high in the air and
turning somersaults on the trampoline.

'Look at Josie!' said Topsy, as Josie swung from bar to bar, like a gymnast on television.

At the end of the class Topsy and Tim
met Liz, the gym instructor. She was
very kind.
'Would Topsy and Tim like to join my
beginners' class after school on
Wednesdays?' she asked Mummy.
'Yes please!' said Topsy and Tim.

After school on Wednesday, Topsy and Tim rushed home to change into their gym kit.
'I can't find my plimsolls!' called Tim.
'Where's my T-shirt?' called Topsy.
At last they were ready.

Several of Topsy and Tim's school friends belonged to the Gym Club already.
'Hello, Andy! Hello, Kerry! We're joining the beginners' class,' said Tim.
They all went into the gym together.

'Who will help get the mats out?' called
Liz. All the children helped to put them
in place.
Kerry turned cartwheels on the mats.
'I'm going to do that soon,' Topsy said
to Liz.

'First we'll start with some warm-up
exercises,' said Liz. 'Stand on your
tiptoes, arms stretched up high.'
Topsy and Tim wobbled a bit at first.
'Now jump in the air, like a rocket,'
said Liz. 'Well done, Topsy and Tim!'

Liz made them touch their toes without
bending their knees, hop, skip and
jump, and then jog on the spot.
Topsy and Tim soon felt warmed-up.

Liz had two grown-up helpers called
Josh and Tina. She split the children
into three groups. Topsy and Kerry
were in Josh's group at the balancing
beam. Kerry was good at balancing. She
walked along the beam quite quickly.
When she reached the middle, she stood
on one leg.

Topsy went along the beam very slowly
and she wobbled a lot.
'Stretch your arms out sideways,' said
Josh. 'It'll help you to balance.'
Topsy reached the end of the beam
without falling off.
'Well done,' said Josh.

Tim and Andy were in Tina's group at the box. Andy went first. He ran, jumped on to the box hands first, and then on to the bouncy mat. He turned a somersault and stood up, arms outstretched.

'Very good, Andy,' said Tina.

When it was Tim's turn, Tina stood by
the box and helped him to jump on.
'It's not as easy as it looks, she said.
Tim landed safely on the bouncy mat.
Instead of doing a somersault, he
bounced as high as he could.
'It's like a trampoline,' he said.

When all the children in Tim's group
had jumped over the box three times,
Liz blew a whistle.
'Each group move on,' she said. Tim's
group went to the balancing bar.
Topsy's group went over to Liz at the
high bars.

'These are called the asymmetric bars,' said Liz to Topsy.
When it was Topsy's turn, Liz lifted her up and Topsy held tight to the bottom bar with both hands. Then she swung backwards and forwards, higher and higher. Topsy felt like a real athlete.

Topsy and Tim liked all the apparatus,
but Tim liked the trampoline best of all.
The children went on it one by one.

When everyone had had two turns on
the trampoline, Liz blew her whistle.
'Time for the floor exercises,' she said.
'We'll start with handstands.'
With a little help, Topsy and Tim did
some handstands.

'Now we are going to teach you how to do cartwheels,' said Liz.
'Yeah!' said Topsy.
Josh turned cartwheels to show them how it was done. Then all the children had a go.

Topsy tried hard, but her legs would not go up and over.
'Take a little run at it,' Liz told her.
'Then down with one hand, down with the next, legs up and over – and land on your feet.'
They had only five minutes to practise before it was time to go.

All that week Topsy and Tim practised
cartwheels in the garden. Josie came
and helped them.
On Saturday they put on a Gym Show
for Mummy and Dad.
Tim turned somersaults and did a
handstand, but Topsy became the star
of the show when she turned a perfect
cartwheel.

learn to swim

Topsy and Tim were learning to swim.
Mummy took them to the swimming pool
nearly every day.

Mummy helped them put on their swimming things and blow up their armbands.

She put their clothes safely in a locker.

They all had to walk through a
footbath on their way to the pool,
to make sure their feet were clean.

There was a small pool for beginners
like Topsy and Tim. It was full of
happy, noisy children.
'Race you to the water!' shouted
Topsy.

Topsy's feet skidded. Mr Pollack
the swimming instructor rushed
to save her.
'Never run near the pool,' he said.
'The floor is wet and slippery
and it's very hard if you fall and
bang your head.'

Topsy and Tim went down the steps
into the pool. Mummy went in with
them. The water came up to Topsy and
Tim's middles.

They held on to the rail and kicked
as hard as they could. Mummy did get
splashed.
'Keep your legs straight,' she said.

'Now let me see you swim dog-paddle,'
said Mummy. Topsy paddled like a puppy.
Her armbands helped her to float.

Tim paddled hard. He splashed more than
Topsy, but his legs kept sinking.

'Do you think you could swim without your armbands?' asked Mummy.
'Of course,' shouted Tim. 'I'm a champion swimmer.'

First Topsy stood in the water
a few steps from the side. Then
she pushed forward in the water
and dog-paddled to the hand rail.
'Well done Topsy,' said Mummy.
'You can really swim now.'

Then it was Tim's turn. He tried hard . . . but his feet would not float.
'Never mind,' said Mummy. 'You must put your armbands back on.'

'Can I help?' said a kind voice.
It was Mr Pollack the swimming
instructor. He told Tim to bob
right down until the water was
up to his chin.
'Now walk along and pull the water
back with your hands,' he said.

Tim paddled hard with his hands,
then he kicked up and down with his legs.
'Look at me,' he gasped. 'I'm swimming!'
And he really was.

Mummy helped them to get dressed
and dry their hair.
'Won't Dad be surprised when we
tell him we can swim
without our armbands,' said Tim.

Dad was waiting for them
in the snack bar.
'Dad, we can swim!' cried Topsy.
Dad *was* pleased. He pointed to
a poster on the wall.
'There's going to be a swimming
competition,' he said. 'You can
swim in the beginners' race, Topsy
and Tim.'

The next week Dad and Mummy
and Topsy and Tim went to the
big pool for the swimming competition.
There were short races.
There were long races.

There was a race for children
swimming on their backs.
Last of all there was the
beginners' race in the
beginners' pool.

Mr Pollack blew his whistle to start
the race. Topsy swam dog-paddle
as fast as she could.
Tim was left behind—but he knew
what to do.

He bobbed right down in the water
until it reached his chin,
then he paddled hard with his hands
and feet. Everyone cheered as
the children swam slowly across the pool.

Topsy and Tim didn't win the race,
but everyone got a Beginners' Badge
because they had all reached the other
side.

Topsy + Tim

make a new friend

Topsy and Tim were playing in the park
when they met a little girl in a wheelchair.
'Hello,' said Topsy. 'What's your name?'
'I'm Jenny,' said the little girl, shyly.
'We're Topsy and Tim and we're twins,'
said Topsy.

'I like your wheelchair, Jenny,' said Tim.
'What makes it go?'
'Guess,' said Jenny.
'Mmmm – a battery?' guessed Tim.
Jenny laughed. 'No,' she said.
'I turn the wheels with my hands.
I'm very strong.'

Jenny whizzed her wheelchair along
and Topsy and Tim raced after her.
Their mums sat on a bench and watched.
'Careful, Topsy and Tim!' called Mummy.
When it was time to go home, Topsy and Tim
waved goodbye to their new friend.
'See you again soon, Jenny,' called Topsy.

When Topsy and Tim arrived at school on Monday morning, Miss Terry said, 'A new girl is coming to join us today. Her name is Jenny and she uses a wheelchair.'
Topsy and Tim guessed that Jenny might be their friend from the park.

'Why does Jenny use a wheelchair?'
asked Vinda.
'Because her legs don't work properly,'
said Miss Terry. 'When a part of
someone's body or brain doesn't work
properly we say they have a disability.'

'Can anyone think of more disabilities?'
asked Miss Terry.
'My uncle's deaf, so he wears a hearing
aid to help him hear,' said Tony Welch.
'My eyes need glasses to help me see
properly,' said Stevie Dunton.

'Some grown-ups who can't see have a guide dog to help them,' said Topsy. Andy Anderson shut his eyes and tried to walk across the room, but he soon bumped into a table.

Everyone laughed at Andy, except
Miss Terry.
'It's very unkind to laugh at, or to
tease, someone who is different,' said
Miss Terry. 'I hope you children will
never, NEVER do such an unkind thing.'

'We won't,' promised all the children.

When Jenny arrived with her classroom
helper, all the children came to say hello.
Jenny was feeling shy, so she was glad
to see Topsy and Tim's friendly faces.
Miss Terry asked the twins to look after
Jenny as she was new.

Topsy and Tim showed Jenny round
the classroom.
'We keep our things in these drawers,'
said Tim. 'This one is mine.'
One of the drawers had a new label.
It said 'Jenny'.
'Here's my drawer,' said Jenny.

Topsy and Tim took Harriet Hamster
out of her cage to show Jenny.
'Would you like to weigh her?' asked Topsy.
Jenny put Harriet on the scales. 'She weighs
one hundred grammes,' said Tim.

The bell rang and it was time for break.
Kerry held the door wide open for Jenny
and her wheelchair. Topsy and Tim
showed the way to the ramp that led to
the playground. Jenny whizzed down the
ramp in her wheelchair.

After break, Miss Terry said, 'Harriet Hamster has escaped from her cage. Someone left the cage door open.'

'It was Topsy and me,' said Tim sadly. 'We were showing Harriet to Jenny.'

'Everyone, please keep a lookout for Harriet,' said Miss Terry.

It was time to do some number work.
'I've forgotten what four looks like,'
said Topsy.
Jenny wrote a figure 4.
'I remember,' said Topsy.
Jenny was good at numbers.

At lunchtime, all the children
had to go and wash their hands.
'I've got my own special toilet, with
a washbasin,' said Jenny.
She showed it to Topsy and Tim.
'It's big enough for Jenny's wheelchair
too,' explained Sue, the helper.

Afternoon lessons began with PE
and Jenny joined in everything.
She whirled around the hall in her
wheelchair.
'Ouch!' said Andy Anderson. 'Jenny's
wheelchair trod on my toe!'

The afternoon ended quietly, with
Miss Terry reading a story to the children.
They all sat on the carpet, listening – and
Jenny sat on the carpet, too.

Mr Taylor, the head teacher, came into the
classroom to see how Jenny was getting on.
He was surprised to see her empty wheelchair.
'Where is Jenny?' he asked.
'She's here with us,' said Tim, waving
to Mr Taylor.

'Jenny got out of her wheelchair
all by herself,' said Topsy.
'I can get back into my wheelchair
all by myself, too,' said Jenny.
Everyone watched while Jenny wriggled
across the floor and pulled herself up
into her chair. It was hard work and it
took a long time, but in the end she
did it.

'Well done, Jenny!' said Mr Taylor,
and everybody clapped. They all felt
very proud of Jenny.

At hometime, Jenny's mother came into
the classroom. She found Jenny with
a big smile on her face.
'Hello, Mum,' she said. 'This is my drawer
and look what I've found in it.'
Jenny opened her drawer – and up popped
Harriet Hamster.
'Hooray!' shouted Topsy and Tim. 'Jenny's
found Harriet Hamster.'

Topsy + Tim

start school

Topsy and Tim were off to school
after a fantastic summer holiday.
They felt happy and excited.
They walked straight past
their old playgroup.

Topsy and Tim were going to join
the bigger children at the Primary School.
They knew the Primary School was
a cheerful, friendly place.
They had been there already,
on a visit. But Topsy and Tim held hands
as they went through the big gateway.

'Oh, look,' said Tim.
'There's Tony Welch.'
'Hi, Tony!' called Topsy,
but her voice came out
not quite loud enough.

The Primary School was much noisier
than their old playgroup.
Some of the bigger children
did look very big.
Topsy and Tim soon met several
of their old friends, as well as Tony.

Miss Terry was Topsy and Tim's class teacher.

She showed them where to hang their coats and shoe bags. Each peg had a different picture by it.
'Remember your special picture,' said Miss Terry, 'and then you will know your own peg.'

'My peg's got a rabbit like Wiggles,'
said Topsy. Tim's peg had a picture
of a black umbrella.

He wasn't sure he could remember
an old umbrella.
'Girls always get the best things,'
grumbled Tim.

Mummy took Topsy and Tim
into their new classroom.
'There's Tony again,' said Topsy.
They went to see what he was doing.

Tony was busy doing a jigsaw puzzle.
'Would you like to do a jigsaw puzzle,
Topsy and Tim?' said Miss Terry.

Topsy and Tim found plenty of
interesting things to do.
There was sand to dig in and
water for sailing and sploshing.
The home corner had scales that worked.

When they felt like looking at books
and pictures, they sat on the carpet
in the quiet corner. The bell for
playtime seemed to ring too soon.

Miss Terry led the children into the school playground. It was full of big boys and girls all making a noise.

Topsy and Tim stayed close to Miss Terry for a while.

Soon Topsy and Tim were playing happily
with some new friends. Then a big boy
rang a loud bell. Everybody stopped playing
and stood in lines to go back into school.

Dinner was served by two jolly ladies, Mrs Knitting and Mrs Pie. At least, Topsy and Tim thought those were their names. Topsy was astonished to see Tim eat all his greens.

Afternoon school
was more like their
old playgroup.
Miss Terry
gathered all the
children round her.
They sang some
clever songs,
with actions.

When it was time to go home,
Topsy and Tim went to put on
their jackets.
'I can remember my peg picture,'
said Tim proudly. 'It's an umbrella.'
But Tim's peg was empty. Tim was upset.
'Never mind, Tim,' said Miss Terry.
'This often happens. I expect someone
knocked your things down and put them
back on the wrong peg by mistake.'

'Here's your jacket,'
called Andy Anderson.

'Did you enjoy your first day
at big school?' asked Mummy
on the way home.

'Of course we did!' said Topsy and Tim.